What a Week

The Sound of Long E

By Cynthia Klingel and Robert B. Noyed

The Child's World®, Inc.

Everyone had things to do this week.

Dean had to see the doctor this week.

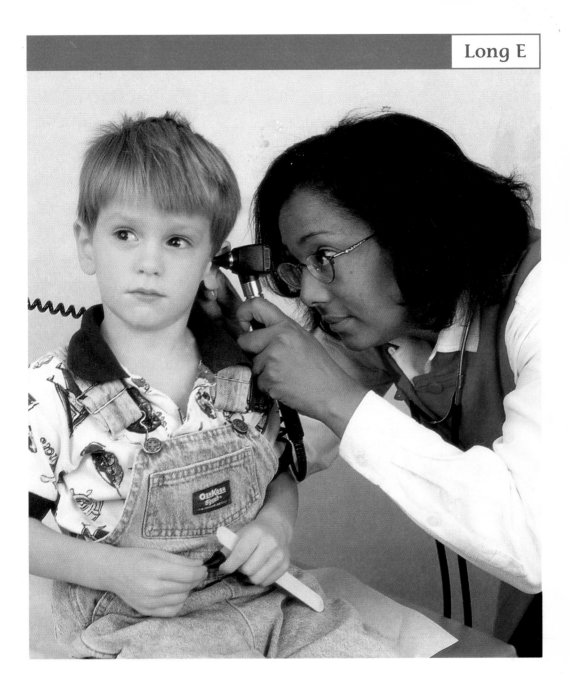

Jean had to clean her room this week.

Steve had to play with his team this week.

Edith had to have a tea party this week.

Pete had to meet his
new teacher this week.

Lena had to plant seeds this week.

Lee had to read a book
this week.

Rena had to feed the cows this week.

What a week! We all needed more sleep.

Word List

clean	needed	sleep
Dean	party	Steve
Edith	Pete	tea
feed	read	teacher
Jean	Rena	team
Lee	see	we
Lena	seeds	week
meet		

Note to Parents and Educators

The books in the Phonics series of the Wonder Books are based on current research which supports the idea that our brains are pattern detectors rather than rules appliers. This means children learn to read easier when they are taught the familiar spelling patterns found in English. As children encounter more complex words, they have greater success in figuring out these words by using the spelling patterns.

Throughout the 35 books, the texts provide the reader with the opportunity to practice and apply knowledge of the sounds in natural language. The 10 books on the long and short vowels introduce the sounds using familiar onsets and rimes, or spelling patterns, for reinforcement. For example, the word "cat" might be used to present the short "a" sound, with the letter "c" being the onset and "-at" being the rime. This approach provides practice and reinforcement of the short "a" sound, as there are many familiar words made with the "-at" rime.

The 21 consonants and the 4 blends ("ch," "sh," "th," and "wh") use many of these same rimes. The letter(s) before the vowel in a word are considered the onset. Changing the onset allows the consonant books in the series to maintain the practice and reinforcement of the rimes. The repeated use of a word or phrase reinforces the target sound.

The numbers on the spine of each the book facilitate arranging the books in the order that children acquire each sound. The books can also be arranged into groups of long vowels, short vowels, consonants, and blends. All the books in each grouping have their numbers printed in the same color on the spine. The books can be grouped and regrouped easily and quickly, depending on the teacher's needs.

The stories and accompanying photographs in this series are based on time-honored concepts in children's literature: Well-written, engaging texts and colorful, high-quality photographs combine to produce books that children want to read again and again.

Dr. Peg Ballard
Mankato State University

Photo Credits

All photos © copyright: Photo Edit: 5 (Michael Newman), 14, 21 (David Young-Wolff); Romie Flanagan/Flanagan Publishing Services: 13, 17, 18; Tony Stone Images: 2 (William Hart), 9 (Lori Adamski Peek), 10 (Sue Ann Miller); Unicorn: 6 (Aneal Vohra). Cover: Romie Flanagan/Flanagan Publishing Services.

An Editorial Directions Book
Photo Research: Alice Flanagan
Design and production: Herman Adler Design Group

Text copyright © 2000 by The Child's World®, Inc.

Library of Congress Cataloging-in-Publication Data

Klingel, Cynthia Fitterer.
    What a week : the sound of "long e" / by Cynthia Klingel and
Robert B. Noyed
    p. cm. — (Wonder books)
    Summary: Simple text and repetition of the letter "e" help readers
learn how to use the "long e" sound.
    ISBN 1-56766-731-7 (lib. bdg. : alk. paper)
    [1. Alphabet.] I. Noyed, Robert B. II. Title. III. Series: Wonder books
(Chanhassen, Minn.)
    PZ7.K6798Wh   1999
    [E]—dc21
                                            99-31937
                                            CIP